CW00859143

The Adventures of Gia and Tiffy: The Girls Meet Their Fairies.

Originally published in the United Kingdom by The Love Heart Club Publishing House, London: 2021.

Part One in *The Adventures of Gia and Tiffy* series.
Originally published in 2021.

Written by Emily Kimber.
Illustrated by Gia Christmas.

The Adventures of

Gia and Tiffy:

The Girls Meet Their Fairies

Chapter One

It's Not Morning Yet

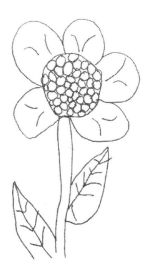

"Gia, Gia. Are you awake?"

Gia rolled over in the bottom bunkbed and slowly opened her eyes. "Yes, I am, Tiffy," she said. "But it's not morning yet."

"It is!" said Tiffy from the top bunk. "Look, open the curtains."

Gia got out of bed, felt a bit of cold air on her arms, put her feet on the wooden floor, and walked to the window. She peaked behind the soft purple curtains, but it was still dark.

"It's still dark," she said to Tiffy who was sitting up in bed, holding Turtle. "You and Turtle need to go back to sleep."

"But I'm not tired," said Tiffy, giving her cuddly toy Turtle a little squeeze.

"Okay," said Gia, walking to the ladder on their bunkbeds. "I'll climb into bed with you and we can plan a magical day."

Gia climbed into Tiffy's bed, said hello to Turtle, then put the pillows behind them to get comfy.

"What do you want to do today?" asked Tiffy.

"I want an adventure at the farm," said Gia, looking up at the ceiling and imagining the warm, lovely feeling she gets whenever she's at the farm.

"You mean Ruby and Grandpa's farm?" asked Tiffy with wide eyes.

"Of course!" said Gia. "We don't know anyone else with a farm."

"But there must be other people with special farms who we haven't met yet," said Tiffy.

"That's true," said Gia. "But right now, we only know about Ruby and Grandpa's farm."

"We'll need to ask Mum and Dad to drive us there," said Tiffy.

"If we need Mum and Dad to take us, we have to wake them up," said Gia.

"But they might be grumpy if we wake them up," said Tiffy. "It's not even morning yet."

"See! It's not morning! I told you," said Gia. "But I have an idea." She shuffled to the side in the bed and now sat facing Tiffy. "What do Mum and Dad like more than anything?"

"Cuddles," said Tiffy.

"No," said Gia.

"Wine?"

"No."

"Breakfast?"

"Closer!"

"Coffee?"

"Yes!" said Gia.

"Yes!" said Tiffy, lifting Turtle in the air and waving him from side to side to celebrate getting the answer right.

"We'll make them coffee," said Gia. "Then they can't be cross when we wake them up."

So, Gia and Tiffy put on their matching fluffy dressing gowns, left Turtle in the bed, and tiptoed quietly down the dark hallway in their flat.

"We need to switch the light on," said Tiffy when they got to the kitchen which was next door to Mum and Dad's room.

"No way," said Gia. "If we do that, we'll wake them up. We need to make them this coffee in the dark. It needs to be a surprise."

"Okay," said Tiffy and they stepped into the pitch-black kitchen, right next door to Mum and Dad's bedroom.

The girls walked over to the low-down cupboards and stood in front of them. But all they could see was black.

"How are we going to find the mugs when we can't see?" asked Tiffy.

"We're just going to have to feel them," said Gia and they crouched down to find the cupboard doors, then both started giggling while they felt around for the handles.

When the cupboards were open, they reached their hands inside, and tried to feel a mug.

"I think I found one," said Tiffy.

"Great," said Gia. "Does it feel like a small bowl with a handle like a mug?"

"Yes," said Tiffy. "I think it might be quite a big mug, though."

"Okay," said Gia. "I think I've found one too, but it's got a long metal handle. That's good we can give this one to Dad."

The girls put the mugs up on the counter by the sink.

"Next we need hot water," said Tiffy.

"You get the hot water and I'll feel for the coffee and put it in these mugs," said Gia, reaching into the high up cupboard where Mum and Dad kept the coffee. She felt something that seemed to be coffee granules. "I can't see what I'm doing in the dark," said Gia, "but I think I've put a teaspoon of coffee in the mugs. It smells a bit funny. I don't like coffee."

"Great," said Tiffy. "Pass them here."

Tiffy found the kitchen sink in the dark, climbed onto a chair so she could reach, and turned on the hot tap. She started filling the mugs with the hot tap water.

"What's that noise?" asked Gia. "Is that the kettle boiling?"

"Erm," said Tiffy, suddenly remembering that Mum and Dad use a kettle to get boiling water, *not* the hot tap.

"Tiffy?"

"Sure, yeah it's the kettle," said Tiffy, hoping that no one would find out she was just using hot water straight from the tap.

"Okay, here you go," said Tiffy, handing Gia one mug and holding onto the other one herself. "Be careful. Don't spill it."

The girls held on carefully to the drinks then slowly tiptoed into Mum and Dad's bedroom.

"Look at them. They look so cute," whispered Tiffy.

"I'll turn the light on," said Gia.

She held her mug with one hand and flicked the switch by their door with the other.

Suddenly bright beaming light filled the entire room.

"Who goes there?!" shouted Mum instantly sitting up in the bed, her eyes wide, and her brown hair messy over her head.

"Mmmmm, what's going on?" muttered Dad, pulling the pillow over his face.

"Oh, girls. It's you," said Mum, looking at Gia and Tiffy standing in their dressing gowns.

"Dan, it's just the girls," said Mum, pulling her hair into a bun. "Wake up, babe, the girls have come in to see us."

"What's that in your hands?" asked Mum while Dad slowly opened his eyes and looked over at them.

"What have you got there?!" asked Dad, sitting up now, too.

Gia and Tiffy looked down. For the first time they could see what they actually had in their hands.

They opened their eyes wide when they saw what it was.

Gia and Tiffy looked at each other. They started giggling. Then they looked back down at their hands.

"What? What is it?" asked Mum.

The girls were now laughing so much their whole bodies were shaking, and they were trying to hold the coffee steady without spilling it while looking at what they had done.

"Erm," said Gia, managing to stop laughing for a minute.

"We tried to make you coffee," said Tiffy with a giggle.

"In a *bowl* and a saucepan?!" asked Dad.

"We couldn't see anything," said Tiffy.

"It was pitch-black," said Gia.

"We didn't want to turn the lights on in case it woke you up," said Tiffy.

"We thought they were mugs," said Gia.

"Oh, girls. It's very sweet," said Mum.

"Bring them here then," said Dad, shaking his head with a big smile. "I'm sure they still taste fine, even in a bowl and saucepan."

Gia and Tiffy brought the drinks onto Mum and Dad's bed and handed them over.

"I'm so sorry," said Gia, trying not to laugh again.

"We really thought we had found mugs," said Tiffy.

"Thank you, darlings," said Mum.

"We want to go to the farm today," said Tiffy.

"We need you to drive us there," said Gia.

"That sounds wonderful," said Mum and took a sip of her coffee from the bowl.

"Sounds good to me," said Dad, looking down at his saucepan then over to Mum.

"You better go and get dressed then," said Mum, after swallowing her coffee with a very confused look on her face.

The girls left and ran down the hallway to their room.

"Did you see Mum's face when she drank that coffee out the bowl?" Tiffy whispered to Gia when they were safely away from Mum and Dad.

"Yeah, she looked like she had just drunk pond water," said Gia. "She did very well to swallow it and not scream."

"Dad didn't touch his one after that," said Tiffy.

"Oh well, at least we get to go to the farm," said Gia. "And we did *try.*"

"Exactly," added Tiffy and both girls began looking in their drawers for some clothes.

They arrived at the farm dressed and ready to play. Gia was wearing purple leopard print leggings, a long black vest, and a dark purple denim jacket. Tiffy was wearing yellow trousers, a matching yellow t-shirt, and a fluffy red cardigan. They ran out of the car as soon as it stopped on the grass and ran across the field.

"Our adventure starts now!" shouted Gia, throwing her arms up in the air and lifting her chin, feeling the warm sun on her face.

"Adventure here we come!" said Tiffy, running as fast as she could, feeling so good.

"I think our adventure should start with the animals," Gia shouted to Tiffy while still running.

"Me too," said Tiffy. "First stop, the donkeys!"

The girls ran over to see the donkeys, who had their own big area of grass next to the goats, while Mum and Dad parked the car.

"Hello Ruby. Hello Mindy," said Tiffy when they got to the donkeys' wooden fence. Ruby the donkey had the same name as their granny Ruby.

"Would you like to come on an adventure with us?" asked Gia, reaching her arm through the fence so she could stroke Mindy's nose.

The donkeys both brayed loudly and nodded their heads.

"Did you see that?" asked Gia. "I think they're saying yes."

"Ask them another question," said Tiffy.

"Can you understand us?" asked Gia.

The donkeys brayed again, and this time Mindy said, "HEE-HAW-YES."

Gia and Tiffy both look at each other with raised eyebrows. Tiffy opened her mouth wide.

"Are you thinking what I'm thinking?" asked Gia.

"The donkeys can talk!" said Tiffy. "Ask them another question."

"Can you talk?" asked Gia.

The donkeys didn't say anything. Gia and Tiffy both frowned.

"Oh well," said Tiffy.

"I guess it was too good to be tru–" Gia started.

But before Gia could finish saying 'true', Ruby shook her head up into the air, gave a quick snort, then looked at the girls and said, "Only when there are no adults to hear us."

Gia and Tiffy gasped then started jumping up and down and hugging each other!

"Shall we tell Mum and Dad?" asked Tiffy when they had finished their celebratory jumps.

"Hmm," said Gia. "Maybe, but not just yet."

"This is so cool," said Tiffy.

"We want you to come to the woods with us," said Mindy.

"But you need to check with your mum and dad first," said Ruby.

"Okay!" said Gia and let out an excited squeal. She could tell their adventure was about to begin.

Chapter Two

We've Got Good News And Bad News

"Mum! Dad!" Gia called as they ran to Mum and Dad who had parked the car by Ruby and

Grandpa's shepherd's hut. They were laying a picnic blanket out on the grass.

"Yes, girls?" Dad answered as they got closer to him.

"We're going to go to the woods," said Gia.

"On your own?" asked Dad.

"Yes," said Tiffy.

"No," said Gia.

Dad laughed. "Well girls, which one is it? Yes or no?"

"We are going without any humans," said Gia.

"We're going with the donkeys," added Tiffy.

Mum and Dad looked at each other.

"It's lunch time now," said Mum. "You need an adult to go with you to the woods, so tell the donkeys they will have to wait until after lunch so that me or Dad can come too."

"The donkeys can't even get out of their fence," said Dad. "They're not like humans at all. They can't climb the gate, can't eat the picnic, and definitely can't talk."

The girls looked at each other.

"You're right," said Gia. She quickly looked at Tiffy when Mum and Dad weren't looking and put her finger on her lips. "Shh," she said.

"Okay," said Tiffy, looking at Dad. "We'll go and tell the donkeys we can't go with them now."

"Good girls," said Mum.

Mum and Dad sat down on the red and black picnic blanket with a cup of tea, then started looking for their favourite sandwiches in the big blue picnic box. Mum was looking for a chicken and salad wrap, and Dad was looking for a peanut butter and jam sandwich on brown bread.

Even though Mum and Dad said they couldn't go to the woods with just the donkeys, the girls were still excited to quickly talk to Ruby and Mindy again before lunch.

"Hello!" said Tiffy as they got nearer.

The donkeys turned around and walked over to meet Gia and Tiffy by the fence again.

"We have good news and bad news," said Tiffy to the donkeys.

"Do we?" asked Gia, raising her voice in surprise. "I thought we only had bad news."

"The *good* news," said Tiffy with a cheeky grin on her face, "is that Mum and Dad think you can't talk."

The two donkeys snorted.

"Why is that good news?" asked Gia.

"Because it means they won't suspect anything," said Tiffy.

"Oh, you mean they'll never guess we're planning an adventure with the donkeys?" asked Gia. "Because how could we if they can't even talk."

"Exactly," said Tiffy.

"So, what's the bad news?" asked Ruby the donkey, shaking her mane, and lifting her front hoofs while she said it.

"We're not allowed to go to the woods with you," said Gia. "We need to take an adult – a *human* adult – with us." Gia stroked Ruby and Mindy's manes, one with each hand, while she told them the news to make them feel better. She thought she could tell what they were thinking when she touched the donkeys' hair or body.

"What are they feeling?" asked Tiffy.

"They're not sad," said Gia. "They're happy. I think they might even be excited."

"Why are you happy?" Tiffy asked looking at Ruby and Mindy.

"We're happy and excited…HEE-HAW," said Mindy.

"…because you don't need us for the first bit of your adventure anyway," finished Ruby and she lifted her front hoofs up again.

"In fact," said Mindy, "the fairies will probably have more fun without us there."

"Hang on," said Gia.

"Yeah, hang on," added Tiffy.

Gia and Tiffy looked at each other.

"Are you thinking what I'm thinking?" asked Tiffy.

Gia slowly nodded her head. The girls turned to face the donkeys.

"Fairies?!" Gia and Tiffy exclaimed at the same time.

"Shh," said Mindy. "The human adults might hear you."

"What fairies?" asked Gia whispering as loudly as she could.

"Fairies, fairies, fairies," said Tiffy jumping up and down, with her hand over her mouth to make her voice quieter.

"Well," said Mindy, "you actually *all* have your own special fairies looking out for you. Every human. All the time."

Gia and Tiffy stood in stunned silence. They didn't know what to say.

"If you go into the woods after lunch," said Ruby, "the fairies will be there to meet you. They are really excited."

"Go to lunch with Mum and Dad first," said Mindy. "Then have fun in the woods with your fairies afterwards. The fairies will be expecting you."

Before the girls could answer they heard something.

"Gia! Tiffy!" It was Mum calling from over by the picnic blanket.

"You better go," whispered Mindy.

"Just one last question," said Tiffy. "How big are the fairies we're looking for?"

"Three of them lying down would fit on a piece of toast," said Ruby with a warm smile.

"Thanks," said Tiffy.

The donkeys ran off away from the fence, braying and swooshing their tails while they ran.

Gia and Tiffy headed back to Mum and Dad and the picnic.

The girls could hardly eat fast enough. Tiffy had tried to shove two sandwiches, a banana, and a handful of Mini Cheddars in her mouth all at the same time, but she started coughing and Mum and Dad stopped her.

"Slow down," said Mum.

"What's the big rush, girls?" asked Dad. "Enjoy your lunch slowly."

But all the girls could think about was finishing the picnic as quickly as possible to get to the woods to meet the fairies – if they even were real, of course.

"I've finished!" said Gia.

Mum looked at Gia's plate. "You've only had one bite!"

Gia looked down. It was true. She had been so distracted by thoughts of the fairies that she had only taken one tiny bite of her sandwich. She couldn't believe it. It felt as though she'd been sat there eating for ages.

Eventually, the picnic was over. It had been nice, but really all Gia and Tiffy could think about was getting to the woods.

Gia and Tiffy stood up on the soft blanket.

"Can we go now?" asked Tiffy.

"Where?" asked Mum.

"Erm, to the woods on our own," said Gia. She said the last bit as quickly as possible, hoping Mum and Dad wouldn't hear what she actually said.

But Mum had heard her. "Only with an adult!"

"Not on your own!" said Dad.

"But Mu-uum," said Tiffy.

"Not that moany voice, Tiff," said Mum.

Gia leant towards Tiffy until their heads were nearly touching and whispered in her ear so that only Tiffy could hear her, "Quick, look cute."

Instantly Gia and Tiffy brought their feet together, leant their heads to one side, held their hands in a prayer shape in front of them, and put on their cutest smiles.

"We love you," said Gia in a sweet, high-pitched voice.

"You're so beautiful," said Tiffy.

Mum and Dad laughed but Gia and Tiffy kept their cute smiles even though their cheeks and lips were starting to ache.

"Hurry up, please," said Tiffy through her fake smile.

"Okay, cutie pies," said Mum. "I guess you can go to the woods on your own. But you must remain where we can see you," she added in a serious voice.

"That is very important," said Dad. "Do not go right into the middle of the woods."

"No problem!" said Gia.

Chapter Three

Tiffy Meets Tiffy And Gia Meets Sofia

Gia and Tiffy got to the edge of the woods and walked onto the muddy area with all the trees. They were more excited than they ever had been before.

"I can't believe we're going to see actual fairies," said Tiffy.

"Well, we *think* we are," said Gia. "We don't know if the donkeys were just making it up."

"I believe in fairies," said Tiffy.

"Me too," said Gia. "But we still don't know if we have our own fairies here in these woods."

"What do they look like?" asked Tiffy.

"Wings," said Gia, shrugging.

"Is that it?" asked Tiffy.

"I'm pretty sure if you saw something with a face and real wings fluttering in the woods you wouldn't need more than that," said Gia.

"What colour are they?" asked Tiffy.

"I don't know," said Gia. "I'm walking with you remember. I don't know more than you do about these fairies."

Just then, in the darkest patch of the woods, which the girls had never stepped into before, they spotted some strange silver lights.

"Look, someone has left some Christmas lights in the woods," said Tiffy.

"Tiffy, are you serious? It's not Christmas, there have never been Christmas lights here, and I think it's the fairies."

"Ahh!" Tiffy screamed with excitement and started doing little spins.

"Shh!" said Gia, trying to be cross but she couldn't help smiling because Tiffy looked so excited. "Let's go," said Gia. She took Tiffy's hand and they slowly started taking steps towards the sparkling lights together.

"Hello," said Tiffy as they got close to the lights.

The girls could see for sure now that these were not lights.

"They are definitely fairies," said Tiffy.

Gia just smiled. Tiffy was right. They *must* be. They were flying, for a start. Lights don't fly. The girls were right next to the fairies now, and they needed to speak again because the fairies hadn't spotted them yet.

"Erm, excuse me, do you speak English?" asked Gia.

The fairies stopped fluttering about and turned around to look at Gia and Tiffy.

The girls gasped.

"Wow. You are the most beautiful fairies I have ever seen," said Gia.

They were also the *only* fairies she had seen, but Gia wasn't going to tell them that.

"Would you like me to do a dance for you?" asked Tiffy.

The fairies started giggling.

"If that would make you happy," said a fairy with a sparkly gold crown and three ponytails.

"Not really," said Gia who wanted to have a proper conversation with them instead. She had so many questions she wanted to ask them.

"Okay!" said Tiffy and did the cutest, most gorgeous, silly dance for them and the fairies all laughed and smiled.

"Thank you," said the fairies when she had finished – all except one fairy who had started dancing at the same time as Tiffy and didn't realise she had stopped.

"You can stop now," said the fairy with three ponytails to the little dancing fairy.

The little dancing fairy spun round and stopped. Then, when she realised everyone was looking at her, she quickly hid her face behind her wings.

"What's your name?" asked Tiffy.

"Tiffy," said the little dancing fairy, slowly moving her wing away.

"I'm called Tiffy, too!" said Tiffy.

"Ah," said the fairy with three ponytails, looking at Tiffy. "Then this is your fairy. Ever since you were born, Tiffy-the-fairy has been looking out for you, getting you ice cream, giving you cool ideas for haircuts, and teaching you lots of lovely songs to sing without you even realising."

"Wow," said Tiffy. "It's so nice to finally meet you. I love you already!" and she gave Tiffy-the-fairy a big hug.

Then Tiffy-the-fairy fluttered up onto Tiffy's shoulder and whispered into her ear, "I can tell you lots of silly jokes, too, and I can get you animals to stroke and ice cream to eat whenever you want it!"

"Not whenever you want it!" said the fairy with three ponytails who had overheard what Tiffy-the-fairy whispered in her ear. "If it's too much ice cream it's not good for you, remember."

"Oh yeah," said Tiffy-the-fairy and her and Tiffy started giggling.

"So, you must be Gia then," said the fairy with three ponytails, flying a little closer to Gia and looking all over her. "We have heard so much about you, and we have been waiting so long to meet you properly like this. I'm Maye, the godmother of all the fairies."

"It's so nice to meet you," said Gia. "Who's my fairy?"

"I am," said a voice from behind the fairies and then out came the most beautiful, calm, peaceful fairy Gia had ever seen. (And she *had* met a few now.) "I'm Sofia," said the fairy and fluttered right up to Gia to give her a little kiss on the cheek.

"Wow," said Gia.

"I've been with you your whole life, too," said Sofia. "I was with you when you were born – you were so excited to come into the world that you were screaming. I was with you in the hospital when you hurt your finger, making sure you were safe and okay all the time. I was with you at every wedding and party and every time you listen to music and dance. I am with you reading books with you whenever you read."

"Thank you," said Gia.

"I will be with you for the rest of your life," said Sofia flying onto Gia's shoulder.

"We each have our own human to look after," said Maye. "Mum and Dad have one too, but adults don't always know it. Aunty Em can see hers sometimes and she is excited that you two are meeting your fairies today. Your aunties and uncles all have their own fairies, too. But not everyone knows we are real."

"What else do you guys do?" asked Gia.

"We make you have fun," said Maye, swooshing her three ponytails around. "Look over there."

Gia looked over to where Maye was pointing. Tiffy and Tiffy-the-fairy were laughing and jumping, splashing in the muddy puddle, giggling every time their legs and bodies got splashed with brown sludge and laughing even harder each time a big lump of mud hit one of them on the face or on their hair.

"Your fairy can show you something good or funny in every single thing that happens to you," said Maye. "The good thing is always there. You just have to look with your fairy and find it."

"Wow," said Gia.

"Once you've met your fairy," Maye continued, "which very few people get to do, it becomes easier to see all the little good things in your life

43

because you are aware of how your fairy is looking at it. And your fairy is only ever looking at it in a good way."

"Well, I definitely have some more questions for you," said Gia, "and you have a lot of explaining to do, but this is good for now."

Sofia fluttered up into the air and back onto Gia's shoulder.

"This is my favourite place to be," said Sofia. "It's very comfy on your shoulder and I like the feeling of your soft hair. Sometimes I hide behind it, too. It's so cosy and warm."

Gia smiled. "Well, you're very welcome to be there all the time," she said. "What do you fairies eat? Do we need to feed you?"

"No," said Sofia. "We're not like pets. We look after ourselves. But we do have one favourite human food."

Sofia looked at Maye and Maye looked at Sofia.

"Toast with butter," said Sofia.

"Mmm," said Maye, closing her eyes and tilting her head back. "So good."

"Do all fairies like toast with butter?" asked Gia.

"It's every fairy's favourite food. We will always find ways to get it," said Sofia with sparkly eyes and a big smile.

"You and Tiffy need to go back to your mum and dad now," said Maye. "They will be wondering where you are. But there's one thing we want to teach you before you go."

"Tiffy!" Gia called. "Come here!"

Tiffy and Tiffy-the-fairy ran and flew over to Gia as fast as their legs and wings would allow them.

"Yes?" asked Tiffy and Tiffy-the-fairy at the same time.

Maye smiled at them, looking at them covered in mud with the happiest grins on their faces.

"Maye has something to tell us before we go," said Gia.

"What is it?" asked Tiffy, her eyes sparkling.

"Well," said Maye, "whatever you want, if you imagine it, and feel good while you imagine it, it will very quickly become real. It's something all humans can do, but most don't know it and it takes a lot of practice."

"Like, *any*thing?" asked Tiffy.

"Anything," said Maye.

"Even telly?" asked Tiffy.

"Definitely telly."

"What about ice cream?"

"Always ice cream."

"What about seeing my friends?"

"Yes, that as well."

"How long does it take?" asked Gia.

"That depends. The thing you want comes whenever you're ready. Whenever you feel the most happy."

"Wow, I'm going to feel happy all the time then!" said Tiffy.

"That is our hope," said Maye.

"Thank you," said Gia. "So all we have to do is think about what we want and feel good while we do it and it will come true?"

"Exactly," said Maye. "Like daydreaming. Now off you go and have a good time. Look after Tiffy-the-fairy and Sofia very well. And remember, once you're out of these woods, no one can see your fairy. You can only see your own fairy. And sometimes you can only *feel* it there."

Tiffy, Tiffy-the-fairy, Gia, and Sofia, ran and flew out of the woods and back over to Mum and Dad's picnic.

"Great news, girls," said Mum. "There's a big rain cloud overhead, about to soak the whole farm, so we're going back to watch telly and eat ice cream. And your Aunties and Ruby are coming with us."

"Yay!" shouted Tiffy jumping up and down.

"That's nice," said Gia.

Tiffy could feel Tiffy-the-fairy dancing on her shoulder and Gia could feel Sofia hug her hair with a big warm smile, totally happy, totally excited, totally safe.

Chapter Four

It's A Dragon... I Love Him!

The lights were off in the girls' bedroom, but their heart shaped night-light was on at the wall and filled the room with a gentle pink glow. Gia and

Tiffy were tucked up in their beds with their soft duvets snuggly over them and, in the low pink light, you could see their fairies sleeping on the pillows with them. It was the most peaceful sight.

The girls had gone to bed very happy after the most perfect evening. There had been telly and ice cream and pizza. At one point there had even been ice cream *on* pizza which Tiffy did but which she said was her fairy's idea which made Gia and Tiffy laugh excitedly and say, "That was such a good idea!"

The adults all thought was Tiffy just playing imagination games when she said it was her fairy. They still didn't know the fairies were real.

Then they'd had the most fun bath time of their lives. All the adults wanted to join in with bubbles and singing and painting on the tiles. The bathroom was so crowded! Mum even got soap bubbles in her hair and tried to blow them off.

"Dan! Help me!" she said, but she was joking, and everyone laughed.

The girls brushed their teeth while they were still in the bath which was way more fun than standing up and doing it by the sink. Sofia had whispered the idea to brush their teeth in the bath to Gia and luckily Mum thought it was a good idea, too. But then Tiffy-the-fairy told Tiffy to spit the toothpaste at the wall and see how much splashed back on them which Mum didn't think was as funny and suddenly the girls were pulled out of the bath, wrapped in towels, and went to pick stories with Aunty Sa and Ruby while Mum and Aunty Em cleaned up the bubbles and the toothpaste in the bathroom.

The girls had five stories – not the most they'd ever had (they once had ten) – but this was special because a different adult read a different book each time. Aunty Sa's story was the best because she read books to children all the time and Aunty Em's was the worst, but it wasn't really her fault because Tiffy had tricked her and given her a washing machine instruction leaflet to read instead of a proper story.

As they fell asleep, whispering for a minute about what a lovely day it was when the adults had left the room, Gia and Tiffy closed their eyes and started imaging things they wanted, just as Maye had said they should, with a warm fluffy feeling of happiness inside them, and finally fell asleep.

It was midnight. Aunty Em and Aunty Sa had got on the train home back to their own houses in London and Ruby had gone back to sleep with the sheep and donkeys and Grandpa on the farm. Mum and Dad were also asleep down the hallway.

Then, the small pink nightlight in the girls' bedroom changed to a big, bright orange light flooding the whole room. It was so bright it woke Gia and Tiffy up.

Gia and Tiffy both started rubbing their eyes, not sure if they were dreaming or if it was morning.

"Are we dreaming or is it morning?" asked Gia, still lying down, saying exactly what Tiffy had just been thinking.

Gia closed her eyes again and pulled the duvet over her head, still feeling sleepy, but Tiffy had rubbed her eyes and sat up straight, wide awake on the top bunk.

"It's not morning and you're not dreaming," said Tiffy.

"What is it then?" asked Gia with her eyes still closed in bed.

"Erm. It's a *dragon*."

Gia immediately opened her eyes and sat up. "Oh my gosh, oh my gosh, oh my gosh," she said, looking at the corner of the room. There really was a dragon there.

It was so big that its head touched the ceiling. Gia quickly rolled out of her bed and climbed up the ladder into Tiffy's bed as fast as she could. She forgot to bring Sofia with her, but Sofia flew right up with her anyway because fairies are always with you even when you forget about them.

"See!" said Tiffy when Gia climbed under the duvet right next to Tiffy. They were now sat up, staring at the dragon in the corner of the room. Tiffy was clutching Turtle.

The dragon had its back to them and was looking at the toys in their toy box. Then it stood up and started looking at the books on their shelves.

"I hate to say it," Gia whispered to Tiffy, not wanting the dragon to hear her, "but why… is there… a dragon… in our room?"

"Well," whispered Tiffy, a very naughty look on her face. "I might have imagined it while I fell asleep last night, just like the fairy in the woods told us to."

"You what?!" gasped Gia, still whispering but a very loud whisper this time. "Why would you make a dragon with your imagination? She meant something nice like candy floss or story time with Dad, not a dragon that breathes fi–"

But before Gia could finish the word 'fire' the dragon spun round, stared directly at them, and a bit of fire whooshed out of its mouth.

Gia and Tiffy froze in fear, staring back at this great big fire-breathing dragon.

"Oops, oops, sorry, sorry," said the dragon in a soft high-pitched voice, batting the little bit of fire away with his hands and blowing three little puffs of air on it to put it out. "That's my bad," he said. "I keep accidentally making fire when I don't mean to. So sorry, so sorry! I'm learning not to do that, but you surprised me. I wasn't expecting to see two girls in here in this room until the morning. I was just looking for some new books to read."

The girls sat staring at the dragon, not blinking, both of their mouths wide open and their eyebrows raised high.

"You're, you're," said Tiffy then stopped.

"You're," Gia tried, then stopped.

"Are you girls okay?" asked the dragon. "You've not really said anything since we met and you're staring at me like you've seen a ghost."

"Like we've just seen a dragon," said Tiffy, quietly.

Gia managed to calm down and focus. She began talking as normally as she could. "I'm sorry, Mr Dragon," she said. "I mean, if that's what we should call you. We will call you whatever you want."

"Yeah, we will call you big blueberry bottom cakes if you want," said Tiffy. "If you don't breathe fire on us!"

"Shh," said Gia, nudging Tiffy in the ribs. "Don't worry, I've got this." Then Gia looked back at the dragon. "Like I was saying, Mr Dragon, we are very happy to see you."

"We think so anyway," whispered Tiffy and felt another hit from Gia under the duvet.

"Very happy," Gia continued. "And you are very welcome here in our room it's just a surprise, that's all, and well, you see, most people use the front door and knock. Do you know what a front door is?" asked Gia.

"Yes, I know what a front door is," said Mr Dragon. "But it was locked so I came in through the wall instead."

"Right," said Gia.

"And I don't know why it's a surprise," said Mr Dragon. "Tiffy imagined me. That's why I'm here."

Tiffy quickly shielded herself with Turtle, in case Gia hit her again. But Gia didn't.

"The thing is my little sister didn't really know what she was doing, and we only just learnt how to create things with our imaginations, and she didn't realise we were only supposed to create good things and..."

But before Gia could finish, Mr Dragon interrupted. "You don't think I'm a good thing?" he asked, suddenly looking very sad.

"No, you're great!" said Tiffy. "A great big fire-breathing dragon!" she added, really excited now, absolutely loving this new dragon in her room. And it didn't even seem to be scary at all.

"You really do seem rather lovely," said Gia. "It's just that, well, you're a dragon, and it's going to be hard to explain you to our mum and dad."

"Look, I know what you humans think of dragons. You think we're all bad and breathe fire and attack people, but most of us are actually really good and because Tiffy created me when she was really happy, she has got the best, kindest, loveliest dragon in the world."

"Yes, we see you're lovely," said Gia, not knowing where to go from here. "It's just that you're still *a dragon.*"

"What are you going to do to me? Kick me out into the street?" Mr Dragon looked as though he was going to cry.

"Could we do that?" asked Gia.

It was Tiffy's turn to hit Gia. "No, Mr Dragon. We would never do that to you," said Tiffy. "You can stay here for*ever!* And you can even have baby dragons here, and lay eggs all over the house, and we can use your fire instead of an oven, and…"

"Tiff! Stop," said Gia. "He's a dragon. Mum and Dad will not let him live in the house."

"But he's my dragon," said Tiffy.

"Yes, I know," said Gia. "But you didn't ask Mum and Dad first."

"Look," said Mr Dragon. "I don't know who your mum and dad are but maybe you could ask them and see if I can stay in the house. I am quite neat and tidy and when I breathe fire it really does warm up the place nicely. I can cook toast in two seconds with my kinda heat!" Mr Dragon did a little dance and another whoosh of flames shot out of his nose. "Oops, oops, oops," he said, batting at the flames again with his hands. "Didn't mean to do that, didn't mean to do that. So sorry, so sorry."

"See," said Gia, whispering to Tiffy. "We can't have him, he's too dangerous." But Gia had felt Sofia do a little happy spin on her shoulder when Mr Dragon mentioned how quickly he could make toast.

"I love him!" said Tiffy loudly, standing up on the top bunk now and jumping off to give him a big hug. "And Tiffy-the-fairy does, too!"

Gia put her head in her hands. "Oh boy," Gia said to herself. "Well, it's going to be fun to see what Mum and Dad have to say about this."

Tiffy was stroking Mr Dragon's big scaly wings and asking him how fast he could fly when Gia had an idea.

"I know," she said, getting Tiffy and Mr Dragon's attention. "Why don't we just hide you until we figure out a nice, lovely place for you to go. A big dragon holiday park, or a beautiful castle with other dragons. There must be some place your type go."

"Lots of dragons aren't nice, though," said Mr Dragon. "But that does sound like a good idea. Just, one thing. How are you going to hide me from your mum and dad?"

"I haven't got the far," said Gia, wondering what on Earth they were going to do.

Chapter Five

Ice Is Dad's Life

It was getting light, which meant morning, which meant Mum and Dad would be up soon and the girls still hadn't figured out what to do. Gia was thinking of plans while Tiffy and Mr Dragon were happily playing with the tea set.

"I've got it!" said Gia eventually. "Mum and Dad only ever come in here when we've done something wrong, when we scream their names for help, when they hear us fight or a big bang, or when we need to get clothes. So, if we get fully dressed now, close the door behind us, and then play nicely in the living room all day, they will never know you're in our bedroom."

"Okay!" said Tiffy. "Come on Mr Dragon, help me get dressed. We're going to play in the living room all day. You'll love it in there, there's a TV in there."

"No, not Mr Dragon," said Gia. "That's the whole point of the plan. Mr Dragon stays hidden in here, so Mum and Dad don't see him, and only *we* go and play in the living room."

Mr Dragon looked sad. So did Tiffy.

"Oh," said Tiffy. "That doesn't sound as fun."

"I know. It's not," said Gia. "But it's a *dragon* and I don't think Mum and Dad will like him as much as we do."

"You like me?" asked Mr Dragon, suddenly smiling and showing his yellow teeth.

"Well, yes actually, I do," said Gia. "I think you seem nice. You're polite, you have beautiful wings, your red eyes are just gorgeous, and you make my little sister happy which, believe it or not, is very important to me. So yes, I do like you. But that doesn't change the fact that you're a dragon and we're not really used to seeing them round here."

Mr Dragon still looked pleased. "Thank you," he said. "And I want you to know that I like you too. Everyone gets to choose whether they see good or bad in everyone and you have chosen to see good in me."

"Yes, well," said Gia. "Oh my gosh!"

"What?!" said Tiffy.

"I think I just heard Mum and Dad."

The girls ran to their bedroom door and quickly closed it, pushing their ears against the door to try and hear if Mum and Dad really were getting up.

"Are the girls still asleep, babe?" Mum asked Dad.

"I don't know, it's quite late," said Dad. "I'll go and check."

"Uh oh," said Tiffy.

"Uh oh," said Gia. "Quick, let's get out of here," she added and her and Tiffy ran out of the room, slamming the door behind them with Mr Dragon now shut alone in the girls' bedroom.

"Hi, girls," said Dad. "I was just coming to check to see if you were awake."

"Yes, we are," said Gia.

"Dad, do you like dragons?" asked Tiffy.

"Tiffy, no!" said Gia crossly, then smiled sweetly at Dad.

"I mean only joking!" said Tiffy, then whispered, "Sorry," to Gia.

"Would you and Mum like a cup of coffee in bed?" asked Gia.

"MU-UM, WOULD YOU LIKE A CUP OF COFFEE IN BED?" shouted Tiffy.

Dad chuckled.

"Ooh, yes please," replied Mum from down the corridor. "But hang on a minute!" she called. "Come here."

The girls walked into Mum and Dad's bedroom and stood in the doorway, trying not to look naughty while they looked at Mum.

"Yes?" asked Gia.

"Last time you made us a hot drink it was because you wanted something," said Mum. "Is there something you want now?"

"No, no not at all," said Gia.

"Nope," said Tiffy, shaking her head.

"Definitely not," Gia added.

"Okay," said Mum, looking at the girls with a small frown. "Then I would love a cup of coffee," she added, changing the frown into a smile.

"Dan! Can you make sure you put the light on in the kitchen and get the girls to use *mugs!*" Mum called.

"Sure, babe," he replied.

"Oh, and Tiffy!" called Mum.

"Yeah?" Tiffy shouted back down the hallway.

"Use water from the *kettle,* not the hot tap."

Tiffy opened her mouth wide and had a very cheeky look on her face. "I don't know what you're talking about, Mum," she said and then ran, giggling, into the kitchen to help Gia and Dad.

The girls and Mum and Dad were all having a lovely morning in the living room. They had been drinking coffee (Mum and Dad) and milk (Gia and Tiffy), eating breakfast, playing games, singing songs, and now they were all snuggled on the sofa watching Frozen while eating popcorn and grapes. The girls had also asked for toast and butter but didn't tell Mum and Dad who it was really for. They kept putting bits of toast on their shoulders when Mum and Dad weren't looking. It was so lovely and normal that the girls had almost totally forgotten about Mr Dragon next door.

Then suddenly there was a crash.

"What was that?!" asked Dad, sitting up straight and looking as though he was about to stand up.

"Nothing, nothing," said Tiffy. "Look, Dad, it's about to be your favourite bit. Christoph is about to say, 'Ice is my liiife'."

"Ice is my life. Ice is my life," Gia and Tiffy started saying together in Christoph's voice to distract Dad and Dad started laughing.

"Phew," Gia whispered to Tiffy. The distraction seemed to have worked.

The girls were a little more nervous than before now while eating their popcorn and watching the movie with Mum and Dad. They could feel their fairies on their shoulders which made them feel more comfortable.

Then, just while Olaf was singing about the summer, there was another big loud crash coming from the girls' bedroom. Gia and Tiffy opened their eyes wide but didn't dare to move.

Dad stood up. "Right, that's it, I'm going to have a look," he said.

"But this is your favourite bit," said Tiffy, trying the same trick again.

"No, it's not," said Dad.

"It's no-one's favourite bit," said Mum. "I think you had better go and look," she added.

The girls jumped up off the sofa and ran to their closed bedroom door, blocking Dad from being able to get in.

"We'll do it," said Gia.

"Yeah," said Tiff. "We'll sort out Mr Dra- I mean, whatever's making that noise. You just go and finish watching Frozen with Mum."

"That's kind, Tiffy. But I think I'll have a look."

And before the girls could come up with another plan Dad pushed past them and walked straight through the doorway.

"WHAT THE BLITHERING BLOOMIN HECK! BABE COME HERE NOW!" shouted Dad.

The girls were standing still like statues staring at the same thing Dad was staring at. Mum had run in to join them and could see it, too: a dragon, sitting on his own in the middle of the room, so big his head touched the ceiling, picking up a piece of bread, one at a time, then blowing a little fire on it, and placing it next to the tea set as toast.

"What*ever* is going on here?" asked Mum.

"Tiffy-the-fairy and Sofia must have asked him to do this," Tiffy whispered to Gia.

"Oh, hi," said Mr Dragon looking at Mum and Dad. "So, the girls told you about me and you were fine with it?"

"No," said Tiffy.

"Not exactly," said Gia.

"Ah," said Mr Dragon putting the toast he had just made down on the wooden floor by his feet. "Just like always then," he added sadly. "More humans who are not happy to see me." He closed his eyes and two tears fell from each one.

"Oh, Mr Dragon!" said Gia.

"It's okay. I get it," said Mr Dragon to Gia in a very sad voice, wiping the tears from his eyes.

"No! Not that!" said Gia. "The piece of toast you just made is on fire!"

"Oh goodness!" said Mum looking at the flaming bread. "Put it out!"

"Oh no, oh no!" said Mr Dragon and he got the glass of water and poured it all out over the toast and onto the floor.

"That's one way to do it," muttered Dad, then looked up at Mr Dragon. "Hi, I'm Dan," he said. "We're a little surprised to see you, but not because you don't seem erm… lovely… because you do… but just… erm… we weren't expecting a guest."

"What are you talking about? It's a dragon, get it out!" said Mum.

"It's a *dragon.* I don't want it to get angry," said Dad.

"Okay guys," said Tiffy standing right by Mr Dragon and facing Mum, Dad, and Gia. "This is my dragon and I made him, and I love him and we're keeping him and we're going to treat him so lovely like a princess and that's that." With the last word Tiffy folded her arms across her chest and stood staring at Mum, Dad and Gia in front of her with her chin held high.

"Thank you," Mr Dragon whispered in Tiffy's ear.

"No problem," she whispered back, then went back to staring at Mum and Dad, waiting for their response.

"Well, we will have to take him to the vet," said Mum.

"Make sure he's clean and see what food he likes," added Dad. "And I don't know what we'll do about where he sleeps but we'll think of something, and I want to be clear about one more thing. It's only a temporary solution. Dragons are not meant to live in houses, they get tired and bored doing that, so we will take him to the dragon sanctuary next week. There's one I know in Whitby."

"How do you know about that?" asked Gia.

"Well," said Mum looking nervously at Dad.

"It's okay," said Dad. "Tell them."

"Well, when I was a little girl," said Mum, "I did the same thing. And my mum, Ruby, made me take the dragon to the same place."

The girls were staring at Mum. She had made a dragon, too!

Dad put his hand on Mum's shoulder.

"It will be quite nice to see Bertie again actually," Mum continued. "That's what he was called. We'll see him when we take Mr Dragon there next week."

"That would be wonderful," said Mr Dragon.

"That's a great plan, Mum," said Gia.

"Yes, I *suppose* I can work with that," said Tiffy. "As long as I get this week with Mr Dragon first."

"Okay, we're good all around, then," said Dad. "And I'll let Aunty Ruth know that we'll be up in Whitby. We can visit her and the boys while we're there."

"Yay!" said Mr Dragon and got so excited that another bit of fire shot out of his mouth and the whole bag of bread next to him set on fire.

Mum gasped.

"Don't worry!" shouted Dad, and ran to the kitchen, grabbed something from the freezer, then ran back in and threw ice cubes onto the flames, instantly putting the fire out. "Ice is my LII-IIIFE!" he said.

And they all laughed.

Chapter Six

The Last Week With Mr Dragon

They had a wonderful week with Mr Dragon. Mum and Dad explained to the girls that they shouldn't tell lots of people about Mr Dragon but added that it didn't matter too much as most people wouldn't believe them anyway. They played games and had pizza every night for a week, and extra toast with butter at every meal, which Mr Dragon cooked in two seconds every time. One night Gia created the most beautiful golden dresses for her, Tiffy, and Mr Dragon while she slept using her imagination the way the fairies had taught her, and the girls made up songs with Mr Dragon, Tiffy-the-fairy, and Sofia. They played wonderful games together while Mum and Dad laughed and drank coffee and read books in the other room.

"Sofia," Gia said to her fairy at the end of the week. It was the morning that they were going to drive Mr Dragon up to the dragon farm in Whitby and leave him there, and Gia and Sofia were alone in the bathroom while Gia brushed her teeth. "You see how Mr Dragon is a nice dragon, well, would a dragon I created always be nice?"

Sofia smiled. "Mr Dragon was very correct when he said to you that you get to choose what you see," said Sofia. "Deep in your hearts, you and Tiffy wanted this to be a nice dragon, and so that was what you saw and that what he was to you. You also deep down wanted your mum and dad to be happy about it and share in the secret with you, and so that happened as well."

"Wow," said Gia. "Creating things with your imagination is really fun."

"Remember, I'm always here to help you, even when you can't see me," said Sofia. "I will always help you find, and see, and feel the good things in everything."

"That's wonderful," said Gia. "So, one more thing…"

"Yes?"

"Can you help me see the good in Tiffy's very loud singing in the car while we drive all the way to Whitby?"

"Yes!" said Sofia while doing a happy little spin in Gia's long, silky hair, then held on tight while Gia spat the toothpaste into the sink.

"Good spit," said Tiffy, who just appeared in the doorway, and smiled at her big sister with Tiffy-the-fairy dancing on her head.

"Thanks," said Gia. "Come on, let's go."

When they arrived in Whitby, they said goodbye to Mr Dragon with lots of hugs and strokes. They looked around the huge castle in Whitby at all the places he would be able to play and met some of the other dragons he would be able to play with. While the girls settled Mr Dragon into his new home, Mum met up with Bertie on the edge of the cliff. She sat with him and Dad and had a coffee, which Bertie heated up in two seconds when it went cold.

After the final goodbyes, they went to visit Aunty Ruth, Uncle Alan, and their cousins Theo and

Louie who all lived together in Whitby on top of a beautiful, magical hill.

The kids were sat at one end of the kitchen table finishing their fishfingers and chips while the adults chatted at the other end.

"We don't just have a dragon," Gia said to Theo who couldn't believe that the girls had really made one. "We also have fairies."

"What?!" gasped Theo, and nearly spat out all of his drink.

"It's really true," said Tiffy. "While we're here, maybe we can get you to meet yours."

"That would be so cool," said Theo. "How do we do it?"

"Well," said Gia. "We're here for the whole weekend, so perhaps it will happen if we plan another adventure…"

Theo smiled. "Doesn't that sound cool, Louie?"

"Yeah," said Louie.

Gia took a quick look at the adults to see if they had heard her. But they were busy talking amongst themselves.

"This sounds like the start of adventure number two," said Tiffy with sparkly eyes.

"I can't wait!" said Gia.

THE END.

Read the next book in the series, The Girls Go To Whitby, to find out what happens in their next adventure.

Printed in Great Britain
by Amazon